This book is dedicated to Betsy Hines Barker,
who searched for books about seeds, caterpillars,
and eggs for her grandchildren. This tale has a
little about each of those natural wonders and, of
course, how they changed Pig's life.

Henry Holt and Company, LLC, *Publishers since 1866*
115 West 18th Street, New York, New York 10011

Henry Holt is a registered trademark
of Henry Holt and Company, LLC

Published in Canada by Fitzhenry & Whiteside Ltd.,
195 Allstate Parkway, Markham, Ontario L3R 4T8.

Library of Congress Cataloging-in-Publication Data
Chorao, Kay.
Pig and Crow / Kay Chorao.
Summary: Crow tricks Pig by trading him supposedly magic items for food,
but in the process Pig discovers the value of hard work, patience, and an
appreciation for beauty and joy.
[1. Barter—Fiction. 2. Pigs—Fiction. 3. Crows—Fiction.
4. Conduct of life—Fiction.] I. Title.
PZ7.C4463Pi 2000 [E]—dc21 99-31776

ISBN 0-8050-5863-X / First Edition—2000
Designed by Nicole Stanco
Printed in the United States of America on acid-free paper. ∞
10 9 8 7 6 5 4 3 2 1
The artist used gouache with ink on watercolor paper
to create the illustrations for this book.

Kay Chorao

PIG and CROW

HENRY HOLT AND COMPANY · NEW YORK

 ig was lonely, but baking raised his spirits.

He baked a lot.

One day Pig baked his favorite chocolate swirl fudge cake.

He set it on the windowsill to cool.

Crow came and perched next to the cake.

"I will give you magic seeds for that cake," said Crow.

He placed a lumpy bundle on the windowsill.

"I do not believe in magic," said Pig.

"These seeds take away loneliness, especially from lonely pigs," said Crow, cocking his head.

Everyone knew how sly Crow was.

"You are fooling me," said Pig. "I won't trade."

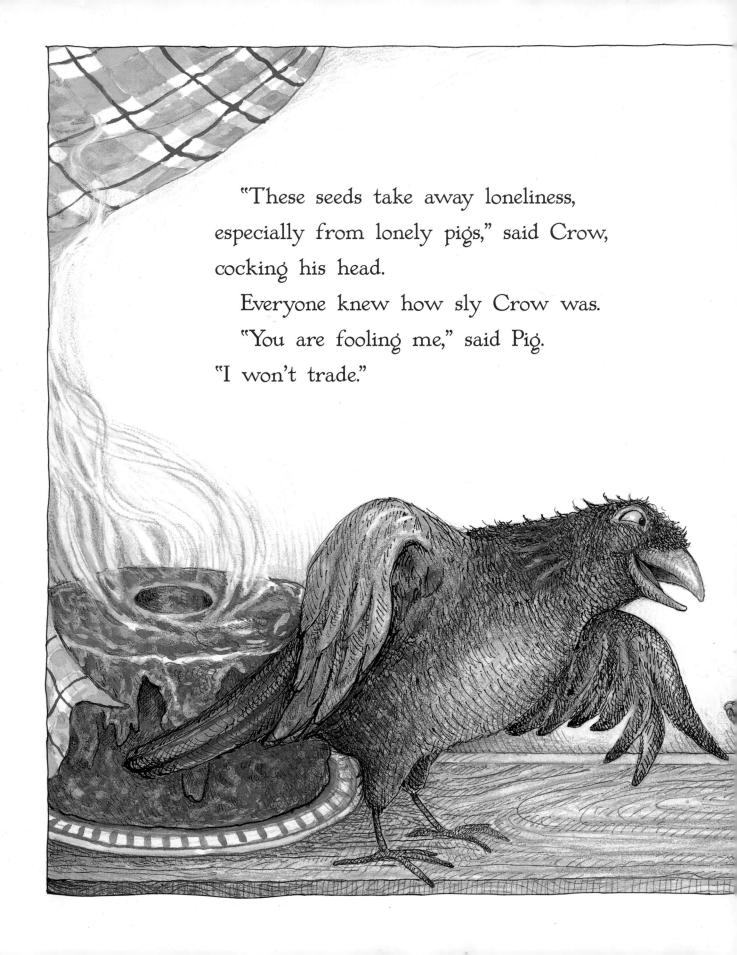

"A pity. Now you will be lonely forever and ever," said Crow.

Pig looked at the little bundle of seeds. Maybe Crow is telling the truth, he thought.

So Crow flew away with the
cake, and Pig untied the bundle.
Out dropped dozens of pale flat seeds and
instructions. The instructions said:

1. To make Magic Seeds work, clear weeds and grass to make a garden.
2. Turn the soil.
3. Plant seeds in rows.
4. Cover the seeds with soil.
5. Water.
6. Fertilize.
7. Keep watering.
8. Wait for Magic to happen.

Pig taped the instructions to the refrigerator.

He cleared the weeds and grass, making a big square patch of brown earth.

He turned the soil with his pitchfork. It was hard work.

He planted the seeds and covered them with earth.
Then, he watered and fertilized and watered some more.

Finally, little green sprouts appeared and, before long,
vines and large leaves and big yellow flowers. Soon, the
flowers withered, leaving small green balls.

Pig kept watering.

The little balls grew larger and larger. They turned
bright orange.

Pig had fine fat pumpkins.

"But they are only pumpkins. They are not magic. I am lonely again," said Pig.

To comfort himself, he baked a pie. It was a spicy walnut pumpkin pie.

He set it on the windowsill to cool.

Crow smelled Pig's pie.

He flew down with a little worm in his beak.

"I will trade you this magic worm for that pie," said Crow.

"Of course not," said Pig.

"You look like a lonely pig. This worm takes away loneliness," said Crow.

"You fooled me once. You will not fool me again," said Pig.

"Well, if you want to be lonely forever and ever I will take my magic worm and fly away," said Crow, cocking his head.

Pig looked at the worm. Hmm, he thought. That worm does look different. It is not pink and slippery like the worms in my garden. Maybe it *is* a magic worm.

So Crow flew away with the pie, and Pig found a list of instructions next to the little worm.

The instructions said:

1. Keep worm in jar with airholes in lid.
2. Feed worm lots of fresh wild cherry leaves.
3. Keep the jar clean.
4. Wait for MAGIC to happen.

Pig found an empty olive jar and put the worm inside.

"I will call you Olive," said Pig.

He fed Olive lots of fresh wild cherry leaves and patiently kept the little worm's home clean.

Pig didn't feel quite so lonely anymore.

But one day Pig found the jar empty, except for some half-eaten leaves and a strange brown lump that was hanging from a twig.

"Crow fooled me again," said Pig. "But how did Olive escape?"

Pig was puzzled.

Every now and then he looked inside the jar for Olive.

It was lonely without her.

One day when Pig peered inside the jar, he saw
a strange thing.

The brown lump shivered. It began to open.

Out came a little black head with antennae.
"Olive?" whispered Pig.

The antennae quivered. Out popped a wing, then
another wing. The lumpy brown shell fell away,
like an outgrown coat. A little creature with damp
wings emerged.

"Olive?" Pig repeated.

The wings unfurled and the creature instantly
became a beautiful butterfly.

"Olive!" said Pig.

He danced around the room. Olive fluttered
delicately through Pig's legs and around his head.

Pig was very happy.

To celebrate, he baked his best apple-raisin bread pudding.

He opened the window wide and set the pudding on the windowsill to cool.

"We will have a party and even invite Crow," said Pig.

The butterfly dipped and twirled and drifted past Pig's ear and glided out the open window.

"Olive, come back, come back!" cried Pig. Tears rolled down his cheeks.

Crow smelled cinnamon and apple.

He swooped down to the windowsill, carrying a large egg.

"I will trade this magic egg for that bread pudding," said Crow.

"No," said Pig. "You fooled me twice. You will not fool me again."

"Well," said Crow, "you look very sad. I would say you are lonelier than ever. This egg will change all that." He cocked his head and looked straight into Pig's sad eyes.

"You are right, Crow. I am even too sad to eat. Take my bread pudding."

Crow flew away with the pudding, and Pig found the instruction under the egg. This time it was very simple:

To make MAGIC work, Keep egg safe and warm.

Pig wrapped the egg in some old flannel pajamas. He kept it safe and warm.

He waited and waited and waited.

"Waiting is a very lonely thing to do," said Pig. "Crow really fooled me this time."

Then one day while Pig was sweeping the floor, he heard a little sound. *Tap, tap, tap.*

"Crow must be hungry again, tapping at my window," said Pig.

But Crow was not outside the window.

Tap, tap, tap.

The sound came from under Pig's old flannel pajamas.

"I had almost forgotten," said Pig.

He unwrapped the egg and saw it had a tiny crack. The crack soon became a little hole. The little hole soon became a big hole.

A fuzzy yellow head poked out, followed by a long neck, skinny wings, a fuzzy body, and big, awkward feet.

"Oh," said Pig, "are you a baby Canada goose?"

The baby toppled and rested for a bit. When it was strong enough, it stood up and honked, "Yes, I am."

From that day on, Pig was very busy caring for
the little goose. It was hard work, but Pig had learned
about hard work from tending his seeds.

It took patience, but Pig had learned patience caring for his little Olive worm.

It took wisdom to appreciate the joy of special moments, but Pig had learned wisdom from Olive Butterfly.

Under Pig's care Goose grew and grew.
After Goose had finished growing, he spread
his wings and showed Pig the wide world.

Pig showed Goose how to cook and garden.

Goose showed Pig how to swim.

Together, they sometimes invited Crow to dinner.

One night after the three had enjoyed a delicious meal, Crow flapped his large black wings and disappeared into the great dark sky. Pig turned to Goose.

"Crow tried to fool me," said Pig, "but his trades really *were* magic."

"Better magic than he ever dreamed of," said Goose.

The two friends stood side by side. They stared into the starry sky for a very long time.

And Pig was never lonely again.